Vampires Are Not Bad

....

Kaya Tish

Contents

Dad (1) — 1

Charlotte's Gang (2) — 3

The biscuit tin (3) — 5

The new girl (4) — 7

Zelvena (5) — 10

My only friend is a VAMPIRE (6) — 13

A world of magic (7) — 16

Decisions (8) — 19

The Vampire World (9) — 22

Vellasette(10) — 25

Telling Dad(11) — 28

Checking in(12) — 31

Roza(13) — 34

Explore(14) — 37

Sattrick(15) — 40

The vampire food(16)   43

Soon (17)   46

Enough(18)   49

Chaos (19)   52

Dad ①

So it's 3:08 am and I'm laid here in this stupid bed , awake because I can't sleep because I know as soon as I fall asleep , even just for a second , dad is going to burst through the door , drunk . Every single night ! He stinks of alcohol , but I don't say anything , no I say absolutely nothing because I know if I do then one day he just won't come back...The door handle shakes and I can just feel the anger flowing from behind the front door, he shoves the key in and violently slams it open , banging into the wall , he stares at me with his bloodshot eyes . I stand there hopelessly pretending I'm invisible or at least praying he won't shout "The hell are you doing up Holly?! " he shouts , right up in my face . The smell of alcohol and cigarettes just flood around the hall way ." I C-can't sleep dad I was just going to get a d-drink" I murmur. He smiles , not a pretty smile not a reassuring smile . A smile that reveals his crooked yellow teeth and when he does so the smell of alchohol becomes so strong I cough and once I do I can't stop so I just stand there coughing my guts out right infront of him. "You trying to say my breath stinks or something? " he asks I shake my head "Go to bed , I don't need little brats like you running about the house while I'm trying to watch telly""But dad you promised you'd help me with my homework""Do I look like I have time to do stupid paper work?!" He shouts his hands are red and cold and are gripping tightly to a chair to try and hide his anger "But dad you promised me!""BED!" He screams I feel the tears coming up now , I hate crying in front of him it makes me feel stupid but I can't help it , but by now I'm crying the tears roll down my cheeks and drop onto my pyjama top. He stands there shaking a little out of anger , glaring at me. I look at him I look at his hair , it used to be a beautiful bronze colour and now it seems like all of the colour has been drained , his eyes look tired how sad and angry he is through them , he stands wearing his green jumper , the one mum bought him before she left that's when it all went wrong . When mum left. I wipe my tears and go upstairs , throw myself into my bed and cry , I don't know how long for but my pillow was practically soaked by the time I'd finished . I just stared at my self in the mirror , I put my hands on my cold tear stained cheeks and wiped any last tears away .

Charlotte's Gang (2)

So I wake up it's Tuesday you can tell I've been crying because my face is still red and my eyes look like they couldn't possible be able to cry anymore , thank god for make up . I do my hair up into a bun and try my best to do some eye shadow, foundation and lipstick . Dads asleep or so I think he won't wake up until lunch time . I drag some uniform out of my wardrobe and put it on . My schools uniform isn't very interesting when I think about it , black skirt , white shirt , green tie , green badge I think it's a book but I'm not too sure . And a black blazer . I grab my bag , sling it over my shoulder and just stand there for a minute , thinking wouldn't it be great if there was someone that actually cares about me enough to knock on my door and walk with me. to school . Yeah , I wish . I arrive at school and get through the large metal gates without being stopped for my uniform checking , then I see them . UGH Charlottes Gang : Charlotte , Rosie , Mia and Lilly . The four most popular girls in school , they are dressed like dolls , so much make up on their faces you can't even tell if they are happy or sad. But Charlotte is the worst , she hates me , which is just great , she walks over with her hair tumbling down her shoulders , bright blonde and she pouts with pure ruby red lips . "Hey you ! LONER! Ugly one?! IT? Thing?!" Her voice becomes louder and soon she's right infront of me judging me with her sapphire blue eyes . "What " I sigh "Hm you look even more trampy then you did yesterday " she laughs and the whole group copies her as if they practice it in their spare time , laughing on cue "Don't you have anything better to do then bully people?! " I shout getting annoyed "Oh look girls , Brat face is getting annoyed ! Keep your wig on !" Again the laugh on cue All of a sudden I see this pale smooth hand reach right over to my head where she grabs the biggest chunk of my hair she can and violently starts shaking it about , my bun collapses , my eyes make up smudges everywhere and she continues to try and rip the hair out of my head . My heads burning . SO bad . It all happened so fast and then the next minute she's stood back again where we was. She smirks and walks of and her little "Gang " walk behind her . They laugh as they walk of , you know one of those stupid girls giggles . And so I'm left there all alone , near the entrance of school , my hairs all over the place , it's like I haven't even brushed it , and there's Make up smudged all over my face and to top it all of the kids that are just arriving go past and laugh at me . I'm just stood there frozen , don't know what to do don't know what to say . I pull the bobble out of my hair , stuff it into my bag and walk to the toilets to wash all my make up off

School drags as usual , at lunch I find somewhere that people won't laugh at me when they go past . It's cold but it's quiet and that's all I care about .

I finally get home and go in , dads not here , he's probably at his job , a part time job of someone who works on the till at our corner shop . He does try , I guess it would be hard on your own . The drinking Dosent help though . I make my self a cup of tea and sit down at the table when there's a knock at the door , I unlock it and see Charlotte standing there , and she is not looking happy

The biscuit tin (3)

"Where is it ?!" Charlotte screamed "Where's what?! " I scream back She shoves her perfect hand into my face "my pink diamond nail ?! It must if come off when I pulled your hair , give it too me RIGHT NOW!" She cries and I cannot believe what I'm hearing , I stand there arms folded "If it has , it's your fault , don't pull my hair next time?! " I reply and go to shut the door in my face but she sticks her foot in right at the last second "NO " she cries " GIVE ME IT BACK RIGHT NOW" I open the door to see her standing there looking even more annoyed " how do I know where it is ?!" I shout , she points to a pink sparkly nail in my hair , then pretends to be sick " probably not even worth having now it's been in your manky hair! " she cries and holds her hand out for it . So I take it out slowly and place it on the ground " what are you doing ?! " she shrieks "well as you said , it's not worth having now ?" I reply and crush the pink nail with my shoe , the nail cracks into small sparkly pieces and just lays there on the concrete . I slowly look up at Charlotte she stand there as if any minute she will just wake up and if will of been a dream . No Charlotte this is life , get used to it . I slam the door in her face and walk back and drink the rest of my cup of tea .

Later on dad comes back , he walks through the door and his work boots stomp along the floor , he kicks them off and walks into the kitchen "I have a homework detention tomorrow " I say . Dads face suddenly turns cold and he looks down at me with his bloodshot eyes " WHY THE HELL DIDNT YOU JUST DO THE HOMEWORK HOLLY ?! " he shouts , clearly getting more and more angry "Because dad, I couldn't do it , I asked you for help and you said you couldn't be bothered with stupid paper work"His eyes flicked with pure anger as I use his own words against him , his whole body is still and all I can see is his nostrils breathing in and out angrily. "Mum would of helped me " I say sternly as he glares at me "WELL SHE ISNT HERE IS SHE?!?!?!?! " he screams , the loudest thing I've ever heard him say and the next minute he's so angry he picks up the biscuit tin and launches it at the wall , he's shaking with anger and I'm shaking with fear I can see the anger flowing through his whole body

CRASH! The biscuit tin smashes into tiny pieces near the wall just like charlottes pink nail had cracked . I sand silently and watch I step back slowly not knowing what to do , I know he wouldn't lay a finger on me , that's all it is he's just mad , he has a right to be mad Dosent he?! He turns around and his eyes are filled with tears , tears because he misses mum , tears because he knows that deep down he isn't being the father he can "I'm sorry " he murmurs and his voice breaks , where it breaks because he started to cry again , I feel his sadness in my throat . I keep standing there silently looking at the floor "You deserve so much better , someone who can give you the world , someone who can treat you better holly " "If it means so much to you dad , stand up and be that person , you are my dad. So be therefore me just listen to me and help me out sometimes? That's all I need " I cry He stands there quietly "It's one hour , my detention "He looks at me without any expression on his face and walks out and goes and sits in the living room

The new girl (4)

S chool once again drags , Charlotte wasn't at school today so her little gang looked like seagulls searching about for something to do , I mean they couldn't even bully people alone they needed Charlotte . I skipped lessons I've done it once or twice before no body came looking for me because I'm not one of those people who stick out I'm just a person who makes up numbers I'm just , there. I hide in the German classroom as no one goes there anymore. Some girls who must of been skiving around there ran out , saying they need somewhere better to hide . I think they are in my year, Lucy and Megan? I don't know , I eat my lunch sat with my back against the wall . It's silent but every now and again the trees will scrape along the windows. Eventually after 4 hours the bell rings I grab my bag and walk towards the gates , then I remember , my detention. Ugh!

I went and sat down in a seat and stared at the walls , This was my second detention the first one was for not obeying a teachers orders , well I'm sorry but I refuse to dissect a frog if charlottes my partner because she was ready to flick half of its guts into my face . Anyway there's about 12 boys sat there pulling faces at each other and 8 girls trying to sort out there nails . The hour dragged , and I mean I ended up counting how many blinks I did in a minute I was that bored. But eventually they let us all go , the other kids rushed to get out , like swarms of kids , pulling , scratching and fighting their way out . I stayed back so I didn't get hurt and when they all went , I then began to walk and that's when I saw her

A incredibly pale girl , perhaps a couple of years older then me she stood at the end of the road. She had silky jet black hair that flowed beautifully down . Her eyes were deep brown she had skin the colour of snow , so pale for a second I considered if she was even human. She was dressed in a black long sleeves top that looked as if it was made of lace and a skirt that matched . She worked tough black boots with the laces neatly tied, around her neck was a black necklace without any charm and a bracelet that was silver it had writing on it but I couldn't work out what it said I think it was Roman numerals , a date perhaps? Damn I wish I'd of paid more attention in maths I could have worked it out . She stood like a stature as if she was giving me a second to admire her beauty , which believe me , I was . I walked up to her and she just stared at me , not a nasty stare but just gazing at me with a small sweet smile with her lips closed they were pure black. I carried on walking and soon went slowly passed her. She smelt like cinnamon with a hint of something I couldn't make out , but it was a nice smell . Her eyes followed me I could feel her stare sinking into my back. She whispered something I couldn't quite make out , a calm voice "Excuse me did you just say something ? " I asked and turned around Her eyes lit up a little and she began to speak " I just said it's Holly isn't it , your name ? "She must have seen the panic in my eyes and the fear as she put her pale hand on my shoulder and held it tight enough to reassure me "Oh don't be scared oh god oh god um... I'm new at the school my names zelv- no umm my names daisy? Y-yes daisy ! "She looks scared her self and Takes her hand back of my shoulder For once in my life I said screw the rules there was something about this girl I couldn't help but love I'd only know her 2 seconds "well whoever you are , would you like to come to my house and I don't know maybe just talk with a cup of coffee? " Her eyes flicker again she looks around and then replies"Why not , " and smiles We walk home and I ask her where she's come from "Well it's a dark area , indescribable in fact ..."

Zelvena (5)

I nodded as we arrived at my house , I opened the door and welcomed her in , as predicted dad wasn't here "Woah " she smiled " it's very bright and cheerful " "I guess" I'd never noticed it before but most of the walks were pastel of at least a pretty light colour She smiled and when she did it felt so heart warming no matter how ice cold her skin looked "Are you cold ? I can put the heating on ? "I say and hand over her hot coffee She shakes her head "No I'm fine " she sips the coffee "but this is amazing!! I haven't had coffee in ages hmmmm it's like magic that runs right to my soul " I watched the cup for black lipstick marks when she stopped drinking but there wasn't one , her lips were still pure black and perfect. and when she sipped again I swear I saw her eyes flicked red just for a second! Even less perhaps. But that can't be right can it? Like not really?I looked at her I want to ask her so many questions but at the same time right now she's the closest I have to a friend and I really don't want to mess that up so I just asked one . I didn't know what answer to expect but any answer was good I supposed "Are you human" There was a long silence and she just looked kinda defeated as if all the life and energy had gone. Her eyes kinda lost their sparkle for a while but she still looked so beautiful. "I cannot lie to you Holly " she began "I aren't like the other people at your school I'm not- how do you put it ? - normal " she sighed My mind was all over the place I had a girl in my home who wasn't even human I didn't know what she was or what she can do or anything but for some reason I felt she was safe to be around. I put my heads on my head and rubbed my eyes. "I can't say that I believed you were all human from the start you just seemed so different- not in a bad way! " I said still staring at her beautiful eyes that seemed like the blacks of her eyes were so black they could have passed as being dipped in poison and the brown parts like sweet melted chocolate drizzled all over. "Thanks I guess? " she laughed "I know you have so many questions and in time they shall all be answered holly"

"If your not human , what are you? " I asked "You wouldn't believe me if I told you , Holly do you believe in magic? " I nodded and that wasn't a lie I've always loved the idea of witches and wizards and magical things but this was not something I'd ever expect to see ,my heart was pounding so heart and my palms were dripping in sweat. "Well I guess I kinda come from that stuff I'm not some magical fairy princess though oh god no! " she shook her head " I am a vampire" All the words were going through my head so fast like a tornado messing up everything in my brain I couldn't process anything as it was all going so fast."You must be joking?!" I cried She shook her head "Yeah right! I'm sorry but how the hell am I ment to believe that? "

She stood up and went into the part of the kitchen were there was more space she locked eyes with me and all of a sudden this deep people mist arrose it just appeared around her like some magical shield the mist shone quiet brightly all shades of purples and lilacs and then eventually drifted into nothing

But she wasn't there , well her human vampire body wasn't but her BAT BODY WAS !!!!!! She was kinda a cute little bat and she just fluttered in the air she was still a midnight black colour like her hair and she danced in the air like she'd been doing it for years ... well she probably had. The mist arose again but for some reason it didn't seem as dramatic this time. Again once it had cleared she was now a vampire again.... "my names Zelvena" she said and smiled

My only friend is a VAMPIRE (6)

I just sit there in disbelief THERES A VAMPIRE IN MY HOME "And I'm sorry about but at least you now know my name isn't really daisy " she says " I'm a normal vampire , which means I am a killer you know the kind that suck blood , I was meant to be born evil you know the crave for killing humans, but somehow I don't feel that crave I'm not like the others there's barely any good vampires left in the entire world. "

"That's why I didn't feel threatened by you then? " I ask "You didn't feel scared because- I'm not allowed to tell you that yet " "Great " I sighed sarcastically "how come you enjoy coffee then?""Just because people assume all vampires only enjoy blood doesn't mean to say they do, I mean don't get me wrong you can't beat a goblet of mdragons blood , but coffees good too" "What?! Dragons exist too?" I asked getting more and more freaked out She nodded "yep , sorry"I just gazed out the windows for an second 1. there's a real life vampire in my house.2. Dragons are real 3. She likes coffee?

"But Holly deep down you know you kinda like the idea of magic in the world , real magic" I nodded , how could not there's a whole world of creatures and beings I've only dreamed of!"Yeah your right I guess"

Then I hear a rattle "Oh god oh god oh god !!!! " I cry It's dad at the door he's already put in the key and I can sense him turning it Zelvenas eyes flickerd " I'll be back soon , bye holly " she smiled , again with her lips closed and then she was gone a small amount of purple mist drifted out but that was all Dad walked right in stomping about in his work boots "Why does it smell of cinnamon?" He said quite calmly I shrugged " I dunno I had a cinnamon latte thing earlier? " "Oh right " he said and walked into the room and put on the telly Same old same old right now I'd of gone and done what u could of my homework , take a shower and draw or watch telly or whatever but now I couldn't I just stood there thinking about her , she was so amazing and wonderful but creepy at the same time. I look at dad and he's just attached to the telly. So after the last sip of my coffee I walk upstairs and sit on my bed . I wanted to speak to her again or just be able to communicate with her , the only friend I have and she's a vampire I thought. I don't care what any one else thinks , that's pretty cool .

Can I summon her? Can I call her some how? I guess it's worth a try? "Z-zelvena?" I whispered "Zelvena?" A little louder "Zelvena!" I said almost shouting.

Hm , nothing. Then a purple mist appeared from the corner of my eye I turned around to see her . She stood there perfectly , smiling a little , then she jumped onto my bed."Hey" she smiled "Um hi " I replied "You called?" "I did " "What for " " well I um , I'm not sure" "I know you Holly , it's because you want someone to talk to , a friend , well sure I'd be more then happy to be your friend! So I'd never had a proper friend before I didn't know how it felt to be cared for by a friend and for some reason it made my face light up and my eyes just stared at her in disbelief and without even thinking I just threw myself into her arms and hugged her. I felt her cold icy arms wrap around me and her silky black hair tumble over my shoulders. I let go and took a step back "Sorry " I smiled "Nothing to be sorry for! I bet your s good friend Holly " And that's when she smiled and her black lips revealed pure white glistening teeth as if they weren't even real they were so beautiful and two large fangs stuck down at either side. For most people this would have scared the life out of them but for some reason I was so amazed by it! Actual fangs!!She smiled "Yeah , real fangs , these are natural " Again , in shock I just stare "Wanna go to ummm ... the coffee shop? " I walk halfway down the stairs and look at dad he seems pretty content so I walk back up "Why not " I laugh

A world of magic (7)

"I'm um, I'm going out! " I said to dad "With who?!"he replied sternly "Um " I look at zelvena " a friend? " "Eh fine" dad shouted from the living room "it's 5:30 now I want you back by 8! " "8?! Is that it" I ask "It's that or nothing Holly " I sigh and walk out with zelvena and I watch her as she walks its more as a hover or a flow her feet do touch the ground but only just as if she can float about , well maybe she can. She tucks her hair behind her ears and smiles her bracelet flickers in the sun and that's when I realise , sun?! "Vampires burn in the sun don't they " I ask nervously She nods "usually , yeah but I have protection from it for 3 more years before I have to get a new bracket " "Oh is that what the brackets Roman numerals for ? A date that your protections up? ""Well , there's two dates , one is the protection from the sun and the second is my birthday , I'm a December vampire , I was born on the 1st of December " she smiled I breathed in her gorgeous cinnamon smell, but still couldn't tell what else I could smell , but I thought I'd already asked enough questions for the time being. We arrived the coffee shop and I asked what she would like to drink "well that's so nice of you holly please can I have ummm .... a cinnamon latte please " perhaps that's why she smelt of spices and cinnamon because she drank so much of the stuff, I ordered 2 and paid , then sat down. "So where do you vampires live? " I asked "A special place hidden away from humans

, and all vampires live there , most people expect us to live in old creepy castles I mean some vampires do but most of us live in like this giant house that's invisible to everyone else but vampires, it's complicated , but cool " she sipped her coffee "Oh " I kinda laughed "so are you really coming to my school?" " I'm afraid not , sorry , I'm only here to ask for your help" "My help?" I asked kinda scared "Yeah , our queen has asked for you! I don't know why or what for but as far as I know your pretty special Holly "Right hold on rewind , Me?! Special?! And the VAMPIRE QUEEN wants me ?! For what!!! "Wha-what , there's like 7 billion people in this world and she wants me , I've know you since 3:30 and my whole worlds just changed vampires and dark magic exist !" She gently nudged the hot coffee towards me and gestured for me to drink some which I did.

"Life is about trying magic adventures Holly , let it all sink in"And for a while we just talked about normal girl stuff , school , life anything and it was perfect all so perfect.

Then I looked at my watch

8:43 WHAT?!?!??!?

"OH ZELVENA MY DAD HES GUNNA KILL ME !!!! " Zelvenas eyes flickered and she grabbed hold of my arm and practically flew me home she was so graceful and stunning as she flowed along the path. Within minutes we were stoodAt the doorstep. I could just feel how angry and annoyed he was from outside I knew as soon as I open that he'd be there waiting to yell at me. Zelvena sighed " good luck yeah? I'll see you tomorrow " and then the purple mist appeared and she was gone.

I opened the door slowly and walked in , then he appeared around from the kitchen and walked into the hallway where I was stood."It's 8:47 , I said to be back by 8 " "I know dad I'm sorry I lost track of time" "SHUT UP HOLLY , I DONT WANT TO HEAR IT , GET TO BED OUT OF MY SIGHT , CANT EVEN FOLLOW SIMPLE INSTRUCTIONS ?!

""Dad I said I really am sorry I didn't do it on purp-"" COME BACK AT 8 !!!! WHAT TIME DO YOU COME BACK ?! , 47 MINUTES PAST!! " he was throwing his arms about like he was crazy and his face was red his eyes were angry. This time I said nothing I just stood there."GET TO BED!!! DIDNT YOU HEAR ME " Now I'm getting mad , not furious but mad but I still don't say anything and I stomp up the stairs , go into my room and slam the door as hard as I can. Dads still shouting but I jump onto my bed pick up my pillow and scream as hard as I possibly can into it. I did this for about 3 minutes just pure screaming I didn't feel like crying or feeling sorry for myself I felt like punching anyone who got in my way.

Decisions (8)

The next day when I woke up I threw in my clothes , left all my make up , stuffed my hair up into an extremely messy bun and slammed the door on my way out . School lasted forever , again and thank goodness I didn't have a detention because I might have actually cried. The whole day I could only think about Zelvena and what could get queen want me for? I finally got out of school and walked through the gates , Charlotte was walking right behind me and started kicking me in the back of my leg , her muddy boots left marks on the back of my tights "Stop it , just stop?! " I shout They all laugh and she continues

Then she falls down , into a huge puddled . The mud soaked into her clothes and hair and her make ups completely ruined.Zelvenas stood there and she whispers into my ear " well , I'm not all good " Charlotte slowly stands up panting like a weirdo and slightly shaking she tries her best to wipe the mud of her but I mean there's no chance that's coming out of her white shirt. I can't help but laugh and I'm not talking about a small chuckle I'm talking about a laugh so big that you sound like a pig crossed with a drunk person I mean I snorted a couple of times I was laughing that hard and my belly was aching so bad but I just couldn't help my self I just looked around and everyone was staring at her laughing they didn't even realise there's a pig next to them . I see the fury rise in her eyes but she's so bothered about her appearance she can't pick on me.Zelvenas trying to hide her smile and I look at her I mouth , thank you and she nods . Charlotte walks up the street and soon is out of sight and everyone else has gone too."Your allowed to trip people up then? " I ask "No we are not but as I said I ain't all good" we laugh and walk all the way up to my house together."Truth is , id really like you to come to the vampires world soon , just to visit" I think about dad and how angry he was last night and how mad I was and how much I loved the idea of magic."What about my dad , he'll be so mad if I come home late? " I asked nervously "Well you could ask him to go out again before we go , he might say no because we were late yesterday , but it's worth a shot ?" She smiles and now when she smiles no matter how cold she looks it warms up her face and her eyes sparkle it's so beautiful to watch her emotions change.I nod and walk into my house "Hey dad " I smile he just grunts , sat with a beer watching telly.We both go up the stairs and there's no point trying to sneak her up because dad is so glued to the telly he dosent look at anything else. I look at all my clothes " I wanna wear something good if I'm going to meet her, your queen " I smile , actually getting excited "Well she likes black " zelevena laughs I take out a black top and some jeans this is all I have , I look at her and she smiles "the queen won't mind if your. It dressed formally I think you turning up at all will make her happy " I do my make up so I look like I've made and effort and just brush my hair down.

Okay , here we go "Dad, I'm off out!!" I shout nervously "Are you hell!!!!" He screams "I am , I need to" " I don't care , your staying in your room all night because I can't trust you!" He shouts angrily from the living room I look at Zelevena and she just looks disappointed and that's when I realised out of all the people in this world this Zelevena wants me to see her queen , more importantly , the queen wants to see me."You know what dad , I'm going , I don't know when I'll be back just like you when your out drinking mist nights!!! " He nearly screams and I hear him leap up from his chair and charge out into the hallway. "YOUR NOT GOING ANYWHERE!!!!" He yells right in my face and his breath stinks of beer again. I grab my bag and stare at him "Watch me " I say in a calm voice And before he can lock the door I'm already out of it running down the street zelvenas bat body is following behind me.

The Vampire World (9)

W e run and run down the street as fast as I can go I can hear dads voice slowly fading away and eventually I stop after running so much I couldn't possibly run anymore. "We need to get to the park" zelevana pants as she has turned back into her vampire body."W-why ? " I'm stood with my hands in my knees trying to catch me breath "There are trees there that can hide the purple mist that appears when we travel so know one will know "I nod and we walk down to the park, by now we have got our breath back and we walk to the trees "Are you sure you want to go?" She says "It's a bit late for that isn't it , how does it work , how do we get there? ""Well I tell my mind where I want to go and the purple mist rises and the next minute I'm there, for you , you need to hold my hands tight and it should take us both" I grab her icy hands tight , and she squeezes back. She gives me a big smile and then all of a sudden this deep purple mist arrive around me like thick fog so I ant see zelvenas anymore , I can't feel the breeze from the wind in the park anymore , The mist slowly goes and I'm left stood inside a huge hotel like place in one corner I see a huge number of vampires drinking red wine? Wait oh god no blood , and then in another there's some talking normally and then there's a receptionist and she looks so strict and firm but so beautiful and delicate at the same time. I look around in awe at the beautiful little fairly light draping from all over the ceiling. Zelvena smiles, "This is my home, I get along with most people but I don't really have many close friends but I like to dance " I just stare at everything with my mouth wide open."It's beautiful! " I say

Every single vampire in the entire building must have heard because everyone in sight just glared at me and all of their eyes for a second glowed red " A HUMAN?!" One cried and I looked over scared "I d-don't mean to alarm anyone it's j-just the q-queen wanted to s-see me " I panic I spit the words out faster then I've ever said anything in my life.Loads of them laugh "Like the queen would request to see a human !! " they giggle Suddenly they stopped and all of their heads turned one way

They turned to a beautiful woman who was slowly walking down the gigantic stairway. She wore gorgeous long bronze hair, that was perfectly in place it had been drawn back over the top of her head and then the rest let loose to dance freely over her shoulders, her skin was just the same as zelvenas pure icy white, her eyes where like glistening gems that shone the colour blue. Her lips where in a slight smile and they glowed the colour red , deep blood red as if the blood had stained her lips . It was such a pure red that lit up her whole face. The dress she wore wasn't like zelvenas top and skirt. It was like a midnight black waterfall the dress fitted her perfectly and the Material soon flowed into lace as it got closer to her arms . The bottom half of the dress was still pure black but scattered over it were red jewels that held in place sections of her dress so that it didn't touch the floor. And to top it all of she wore a crown, a crown that was shimmering in the glow of the fairly lights it was tall and covered in red gems and the ends of the crown were like sharp daggers she was so beautifully scary as she slowly came to the end of the steps. She kept a stern face and began to speak in a calm and soft voice that was so lovely I forgot about how dangerous she was and how I should be deeply scared by her presence."Yes Lorcan , I did request to see a human. Ad if you have a problem with that, I suggest you come and see me "Her voice boomed around the entrance and every vampire there was silent.

Vellasette (10)

I didn't move a muscle. She turned and looked at me. "Holly" she smiled so brightly her eyes flickered "How lovely it is too see you again , you have become every so strong and beautiful" "W-we've met? " I whisperShe nods "A very long time ago" I smile , I don't know why but just like with Zelvena I trusted her instantly she seemed so loving but so powerful and deadly at the same time. "As you are aware I am queen of the vampire kind , but you may call me Vellasette and even if that's too much for you , I shall respond to Vella." "Vellasette , it's such a pretty name" I smile still in awe by her beauty She returns the smile "I see you have been brought up with manners Holly" I nod politely. The other vampires are watching as if it's a movie and not one of them dared to make a sound. "You can all get back to what you were doing! , thank you. All except Zelvena and Holly " she shouts and again it echoes around the huge entrance. They slowly get back to whatever they were doing and Vellasette beconed is to follow her , so we did , she led us right up the huge staircase , like a pace staircase that you only see if fairytales , then a long a beautifully lit up corridor and to the door right at the bottom which said in bold writing

VELLASETTE , QUEEN OF THE VAMPIRE KIND

Woah I thought and she opened the door without even touching it. Her office or room or whatever it was , was incredible . It had soft black sofas around with blood red cushions and from the ceiling hung a beautiful chandelier it was black too but from it crystals and diamonds dangled and they sparkled like her eyes. The walls were very modern , they were painted black but had patterns across them I think they were flowers but I couldn't be sure. There was also a huge desk scattered with all sorts of paper work. A cosy chair had been placed next to it. "This is my office , you may come on in and take a seat." She smiled and opened the door a little further and put out her arm to a sofa in the middle.Zelvena and I sat down and watched her. "Zelvena has been talking to you about how she is a good vampire?" She sits down and I nod "Well almost everyone in this building is a dark vampire. In case you are wondering I am neutral and I believe it is up to every vampire to make their own decision "I nod again speechless , I mean what do you do I'm sat in a vampire queens office."But I need your help with something" "W-what could you possibly need me for? " I ask "I want to see how a human would cope in a vampire world, what they do differently, us vampires don't go into your human world unless they are hungry. I would like you to stay a while."I laugh a little."Your kidding right? My dad would kill me if I didn't return home and what about the dark vampires! What if they kill me!" I panick"Holly , I shall not allow them to hurt you and your right your father will be mad but , I know deep down you would love the chance to stay here , deep down you always believed in magic Holly and that's one of the reasons I chose you. "I rub my head and sigh. "How do I tell him? I can't just say oh hey dad I'm just going to live with some vampires for a while" She smiled "No your right you can't say that. But you are staying with Zelvena, so perhaps you could say a friend""He won't let me go" I say "You can do it Holly, you can make him let you go, somehow." She smiles "Zelvena shall return you home and then you can pack your things you shan't need food or water we shall provide everything for you. I suggest you bring something of comfort , what's it called ummm ... oh yes , a teddy bear perhaps. And clothes and whatever else you need . " I turned to Zelvena who was sat there slightly smiling "Your going to love it! "I smile and squeal a little out of excitement "I know!" I laugh Vellasette smiled "Go now and be back soon , good luck " Zelvena took my hands and once again the purple mist arose.

Telling Dad (11)

We arrived home outside my door and once again I could feel the anger bubbling from underneath the door I knew dad was there behind it ready to shout down my throat, he'd had over an hour to prepare his speech. Zelvena looked at me she frowned. I smiled at her."Why are you smiling?" She laughed "Because I'm done with being shouted at I'm going to give him a taste of his own medicine I'm sick of being shouted at , I'm sick of it all. And you being here , you breaking me out of this cycle. I refuse to stand for it." I laugh and I hug her and her icy arms wrap around me again her eyes flicker and she smiles revealing her fangs. "I'll stay out here " she said and stepped back.I grab the handle and yank it down , push it open and walk right in . I quickly smile at Zelvena before I slam the door and walk threw into the kitchen and make myself a drink I heard him come storming out from the living room and stand behind me"The hell do you think your doing lately?! " he shouts "You can't do what you want you cant act how you want you can't , you can't..." I interrupt him "be myself? You want me to be whatever you want I'm not allowed to be different I'm not allowed to be me?" "That's not what I meant Holly!!!!" He shouts."You Follow my rules , you do as your told and from now on you go to bed early! If I ask you to clean , to do your homework you do it!!! And your make up?! I'm throwing it out!!!!! " he snarled. I spat out a lot of my water into the sink and faced him "You do that , and I'll pour every bottle of alchohol you have down the sink , I'll smash the tv up and I'll bin all your clothes! " I shout , and for once in my life I wasn't going to hold back I wasn't going to stop myself I was going to shout until I could shout no more."Don't you are speak to your father like that , your a disgrace to this family Holly!!" I laugh sarcastically "Says the alcoholic " He stands for a minute breathing heavily. There's just silence "I'm sleeping at a friends for a while I'm going to pack some stuff and then I'm going" "I DONT THINK SO , YOUR GOING TO BED!!!!" I look at him , put down my water and go upstairs and start packing my things I pack make up , clothes, my teddy mum got me when I was a baby, he was a little golden bear and I called him moonlight. I used to hug him whenever I was upset. Well I still do. I put him in the suitcase along with everything else I need and zipped it up. Then went back downstairs."What now ?! YOUR MEANT TO BE IN BED!" She shouted I stand near the door with my suitcase "I told you where I was going , to be honest dad I don't think you care where I go or what I do" "Yeah well so what if I don't?! I gave my word to your mother I'd do my best to look after you! ""Your meant to love your daughter , not just pretend you do because you have someone your word!! " He looked angry and stormed back into the room and flung himself back into the sofa and continued watching tv.For a minute I just stood there and realised that I might as well just take this chance to go. I opened the door shouted bye and slammed it behind me.

"Woah" said zelvena "your pretty fiesty and strong when your mad" I laugh , "I guess there's only so much I can take, at least my dad knows where I'm going now and I can finally enjoy my self with you in .... in ? What's it called? ""The vampire world is called Darkveil." She smiled and her eyes flickered black.I look down at my suitcase and at Zelvena "I'll be alright won't I? ""You'll be more then alright , you'll love it. It will be like a huge sleepover with me! ""Dad never let me have sleepovers" I smile a little "Well who cares what he thinks right now , welcome to my world.." she smiled brightly showing over her large icy white fangs " a world of darkness."

Checking in (12)

Eventually we arrived again at the vampire world or as Zelvena called it Darkveil , but this time we didn't arrive inside the huge building we arrived outside it and I glanced round at the vast garden it was covered in pure emerald grass like jewels laid out like a carpet and trees neatly placed in corners there was a water fountain of a wolf that poured beautiful blue water out of its mouth. The sky was bright blue without a cloud insight and Zelvena began to walk toward the large brown doors that were attached to a gigantic castle no wait a palace it was all in stone and had many layers there were steps going up to it and I was stood on them. I was looking up at the palace as Zelvena was opening the door "It isn't locked?" I asked"It's never locked to a vampire" she smiled and beckoned me up the stairs.So I walked in after her and nothing much had changed inside. I tried to take in every detail and I looked at the receptionist again she had a name badge on her desk saying

MEPOLY

Hm that must be her name, I thought and her head jerked up glaring at me. "Zelvena and Holly how lovely it is to see you again. Vellasette is waiting for you in her office." She beamed I just kind of daydream at her she looks just like a normal receptionist. She has short curly blonde hair and blue eyes her lips have been coloured coral pink and she smiled . That's when I was sure she was a vampire as her fangs like everyone else's struck down"Th-thank you" I smiled Her smile widened " your very welcome" I followed Zelvena back up to the queens office. Before she could knock the door swung open and froze just before it hit the wall."Come in" a sweet voice called . Once again I found my self sat in this huge but beautifully decorated room. Vellasette handed me a key "Your room is number 342" she stood with her hands together and with good posture her head held high with a way that made her seem better then everyone , which she was , but she didn't do it in a way that everyone thought she was selfish and nasty , she was just naturally better. " You may unpack all your things in that room and add any decoratio-"I did mean to be rude but I interrupted her "I can decorate it!? " I gasped She stood sternly and for a minute I didn't know what what going to happen whether she was going to be angry or disappointed . But then her stern face turned into a smile"You may express yourself throughout your room yes of course just as any other vampire can... I suppose your father didn't let you do much with your room in the human world?" I shook my head "He is a stubborn soul your father , but that doesn't matter now , this is a new place where rules change and probably much to your liking" She took a sip out of a silver goblet and from what I could tell it was blood of some sort and it was thick I could see it pour into her mouth and when she lowered the cup she licked her red slips capturing any last drops. That was then the door flew open and what looked like a higher up vampire burst in he was dressed In a casual black shirt which was neatly ironed with a black kind of glittery tie his hair was swayed to the right and was deep black it wasn't perfectly combed but still neat. His fangs showed when he spoke "Your majesty! It's Roza! Even though you said she must stay away from the nursery she's tormenting the vampire children , taking there blood bottles and causing chaos! " he chanted The queen rolled her eyes , put her glass down and looked at him."Again?! I gave her orders not to go near the nursery!! And she promised!" The man looked at her " I'm sorry your majesty" She looked at us and I stared back wondering "Follow me girls , I cannot leave you like this"

So we did we walked threw many corridors and beautiful layers of the building until we reached a darker part of the building. A door creaked open and we all walked inside . I was kinda holding onto Zelvenas arm hoping she would give me some more guidance as I couldn't see much. She held my arm tight until eventually we were all standing under some more fairy lights. It looked like a police questioning room and a Young vampire girl around the age of 20 sat there looking angry and annoyed. Vellasette sat down at the seat opposite her while the rest stood near the doorway.

Roza(13)

The girl spat at Vellasette as she sat and slumped into her chair"I refuse to keep out of the nursery Vella! If I want to take the babies bottles so what! Thought you said you wouldn't make people be good or bad thought you said we could choose our own paths" she cackled and glared at the queen deeply her eyes were black like Vellasettes and they were swirling around like a cauldron filled with poison "You do not have permission to call me Vella, I am Your majesty to you, and I do believe that every vampire should choose their own path , but not at the expense of others, taking blood from babies Roza knowing they are defenceless and leaving them to starve? You could have been the darkest most vicious vampire out there. But don't you attack my vampires especially not the children , you find your own victims from outside Darkveil and leave everyone in Darkveil alone. You have had far too many chances Roza you mistook my kindness as weakness and perhaps I was wrong to give you the benefit of the doubt. Do you know how many vampires have begged me to send you away to make you leave Darkveil and never return? Or how many vampires have begged that I just let somebody rip you to shreds and let your black heart be no use?"Roza just sat there her eyes slowly swirled back into their normal colour and she began to bite her nails."Why don't you then?! Why don't you just turn me away... you have a good reason too" she sniffed turning her head away "I don't turn people away Roza, I don't tell people they are worthless and if I did say that to you , I'd be lying! You think I should just give up on you and turn my back?! That's not what makes a leader ... and it's certainly not what makes a queen"A small black tear trickled down Rozas cheek and she wiped it away roughly with her sleeve she looked up at Vellasette who was sat on the chair looking at her and she smiled slightly "Why are you so nice to everyone no matter how nasty they are to you huh? What's the secret" she spat angry and upset "There's no secret Roza! There isn't some magical potion you can just drink and suddenly your patient , its about believing in others and being strong. Showing them that they always have someone and strength to keep yourself going when I was a little vampire Roza my father told me I wasn't good enough for anything , I wasn't strong enough to be a leader" she let out a small chuckle "I showed him!" I smiled because for some reason it made me happy to listen to her stories even though they were all aimed at Roza "And you can show all the other vampires out there that you deserve to be here , that your starting a fresh and if anyone has a problem with that or is trying to bring you down they can come see me" she looked at Roza "Okay?" Roza finally turned her head and looked up at the queen she nodded. She gave one last quick smile which I think was her own way of saying thanks , and left the room. Vellasette just sat there and glared at the table. Zelvena slowly went over and sat in the chair opposite her." Without you , Darkveil would be in tatters , you somehow give everyone the sense of order but at the same time they know they are free. There's something extra ordinary about you your majesty" she smiled Vellasette smiled back "Thank you Zelvena" she got up from the table and tucked her chair in and turned to face me "And I'm incredibly sorry for that interruption Holly, Roza is just-""It's okay your majesty , you don't have to explain anything to me"She nodded "You may call me Vellasette Holly , you have permission" she slowly looked round for any thing left to do in the room and then turned back to me "Well you and Zelvena are more then welcome to look round and enjoy yourselfs and if you want something other to drink then blood there's a normal food and drink cafe near reception" and with that she flowed beautifully out and we all stepped out behind her to catch a glimpse of her slowly walking back up the vast staircase. She was so powerful but the power never went to her head she was such an amazing woman and her talents were used through the role of a queen. She really did give everyone the feeling of order and many rules were laid out but at the same time you were as free as a bird because you could write your own story and be who you wanted...

Explore (14)

S o me and Zelvena started to wonder round I saw all the cafes and there was a whole dance area which I suspect Zelvena Spent a lot of time in everything looked so detailed and incredibly artistic. Then my phone began to buzz.

BZZZZZZ BZZZZZZ BZZZZZZ BZZZZZ I pulled it from my pocket expecting it to be dad but it wasn't .... it was charlotte , the heck does she want? I answer it as Zelvenas just getting two coffees.

"Hey Tramp , it's Charlotte" she boomed down the phone "Your so Lucky the school is paying for my clothes to be properly cleaned , Tomorrow we have maths and you better be waiting outside for me I need your lunch money to put in my purse so that I have enough for the Rose-Gold shimmer stick from Macie's boutique. ""Charlotte you can get lost I gave you what I had on Wednesday! I don't have any more money!! I went without any dinner on Thursday and Friday!""Yeah right whatever you could be on your knees starving and I couldn't give a damn , Listen Freak if you don't meet me outside maths tomorrow the next time I see you? I'll beat you to a pulp my friends and I? We will make sure you can't get up again! It's a good job nobody cares bout weirdos like you ain't it? " she spat nastily down the phone"You know what charlotte? " I look around and see Zelvena talking to the staff at the coffee bar and vampires laughing happily together. For a moment everything seems like paradise. "You start on me? I'll tear you to shreds I'm done playing some scared little victim I ain't going to stand here and let you tell me what I'm doing on Monday. You are not getting no more money from me and if you wanna bring your little gang along to beat me up? Do so because your just some spoilt little brat who thinks she's perfect well news flash HUNNY , your not!!!" I breathing heavily and I'm angry in side in fact I'm pretty furious. By this time Zelvena has understood everything that's happened and says "If she takes you on , she takes me on and good vampire or not . I'll suck every drop of blood out of her until she's nothing but a floppy bit of skin with some bones."

"And charlotte? If you really think I'm making empty threats go ahead try it but I have a friend here and if you simply try and beat me up consider your self dead"

"Really?!" She cackled "and how are you going to beat someone like me up ?! Call me nasty names until I drop dead" she snorted

"No .... my friend will drink your blood" For a second there is was a silence and I was stood there grinning because charlotte may have thought I was just a freak but I'm the freak with a vampire friend.

She started cackling louder and louder "DRINK MY BLOOD?!?! AH-HAHHA. WHAT IS SHE A VAMPIRE?!"

"Yes , yes she is"

"I'll play your silly little game! Come on then I dare you!" She just carried on laughing " next time I see you Holly, your dead""Yeah, you wish"And with that I hung up and shoved my phone back in my pocketI looked at Zelvena who had a calm face and she sipped her coffee "so are we really-""Kill her? Suck her blood? Yes , yes we are but only if she goes to beat you up , but I'm sure she will" I didn't really know what to say so I said nothing and we walked up to all the rooms and we stopped at ours. "Sorry about the mess, I made your bed for you though " she stuck the key into the door and then slowly pushed it open revealing a peaceful room the walls were covered in shades of deep purple Two beds , they were quite high up and neatly made up. The bedding was the same colour as the walls and in another part of the room stood a wardrobe with matched with the to sling with some drawers and some beautiful flowers. And a white counter top against the wall it had a small purple kettle on it with a little white cup filled with Tea , coffee and hot chocolate sachets it was all so beautiful and neat. The longer you stated the more detailed the room became , there were more fairly lights around the beds and a bedside table to separate them with a lamp on it and a remote for the Tv which was up on the wall.

Sattrick(15)

I put my hands over my mouth and just gazed at it all "I decorated it like this but I don't mind if you want to change it"I shook my head quickly"No! This is perfect , it's even better then perfect!" I smile.Everything had happened so fast , have you ever had that feeling where so much has happened in one day? Like you go on holiday and you think an hour ago you where in bed and now your at an airport? And it feels strange? I feel like that a lot here. I feel like I don't want to waste a second as if it's just like a holiday and I'm praying some miracle will happen so that I never have to return home.

Never. Dads only looking after me because he promised mum he would, and now he can do whatever he likes. Even if that is too drink until he passes out.

"I used to be able to watch you at school" zelvena smiled "I wish I could of intervened, I saw the time charlotte threw your bag in the schools pond. And when she tried to drown you in the massive mud puddle outside the maths block and also when she tore all your essay into shreds, and even when she got her friends to try and push you out into the road in front of the school bus, and- woah she really hates you.""Yeah , she does" I sigh "Why?""Because She can everyone else has loads of friends at my school, they all have friends that can back them up when charlotte tries to go for them. But she knows I'm a loner and I've known her for a while so she takes everything out on me and , and over time her hates so strong for me. I'm actually pretty scared and she knows that too."

"I wish I could tell you" she whispered

Now a million things start swirling round my head. Are you friends with her?! Is she moving schools? "What?" I blurt out "Wh-what oh um nothing" she started biting her nails."Zelvena? Tell me what? Please!" She looked at me for a second and then looked away and then back and me and everytime she looked at me I stuck out my pet lip not in a bratty way but just to show her that whatever it was. I'd like to know."Charlotte she's .... she's""She's what?""Vicious , she isn't just a bratty girl Holly she's , evil. A while ago ,Sattrick , he um he's a vamp here. He went out of Darkveil for a break and he wanted to see how you guys lived and he walked past your school and , and Charlotte saw him and she , " there was a tear forming in Zelvenas eyes it was a deep black tear that was now slowly rolling down her cheek. I sat quietly and looked at her trying my best to comfort her with just a facial expression."What Zelvena? What did she do"She sniffed " She dragged him over and called him Goth boy or something that's what I heard, then she said something about how she'd had a bad day because apparently it was like she was invisible and poor Sattrick stood there not knowing what to do or say. So she just beat him up , we found him with a black eye, but she'd punched him so hard and poor Sattrick hadn't come to cause trouble so he didn't retaliate , sure he told her to stop and he shouted.. but soon she had pushed him so he had fell and he smacked his head on the curb and she just left him there , and you see because we can see what's going on in your human world sometimes, thank god somebody had seen it and they got to take him back up to the vampire world but by then it was too late. And Charlotte she just stared at him laughing then went back to whatever she was doing." Zelvena was wiping her tears with her lace sleeve so I got up and gave a tissue from on the side. "Zelvena, I'm so s-sorry" I just stared at the poor vampire girl , my only friend and I didn't know what to say or do part of me felt like somehow I was to blame as if Charlotte was my problem. She shook her head."It's alright , I just , none of us are aloud to touch her unless she threatens your life. We agreed that we still try and keep the peace unless she attempts to hurt someone else and seeing as though your her only target at moment , that somebody was you."

The vampire food (16)

I look at her in disbelief at what's just come out of her mouth, Charlotte killed a Vampire and she's been let of, no consequences , like her whole life. Later on we have dinner it's like a huge restaurant and there's special people cooking up huge big lumps of steak and it looks like really good food. They toss the meat into a big pan for about five seconds , take it out and put it on a plate it's raw like, I don't even think its even warm. But that's the way they like it, and I'm cool with that. I see Vellasette sitting with a few vampires in the corner. She's eating the same as everyone else apart from some vampires who chose different foods of the menu , like pasta and potatos. But most were eating raw meat. Vellasette beckoned me to sit with her. So me and Zelvena quickly walked along the red carpet and up a step to the corner she was eating at. "So glad you could join us Holly!"she smiled and shuffled over so there was room for everyone around the table."It all looks lovely Vellasette" I remembered she had asked me to call her that rather then your majesty , perhaps she wanted to be like the others. She didn't want to be made to feel superior."Yes dear, this is a vampires dinner. Obviously I shan't force you to eat the meat I know many humans are fond of it but it's probably under cooked for your liking." She continued to speak with enthusiasm as if my presence was essential , she seemed so happy to just have me here. And that felt nice, to be wanted. So

I shook my head politely "Yep, im afraid it's a tiny bit raw for me" "Please , please choose something you'd like, anything" and she handed me a menu. So I scanned through it I saw things such as Mild spiced mint lamb Tomato infused curry with a side of tiger bread Fresh panini toasted with hints of paprikaEtc etc it was all so elaborate and I was worried whatever I chose would be a bad choice but then finally beat the end I saw Jacket potato , with cheese. Thank goodness because honestly the herb coveted toast was probably the next best thing."I'll have the jacket potato with cheese please" I smiled politely , she returned the smile "I'm guessing our Vampire delicacies aren't your thing?"I giggled a little but shook my head "They do sound delicious Though!"She laughed again and pretended to whisper "even I wouldn't try the cinnamon prawns with tomato butter" We all laughed for a while and enjoyed dinner. It was the first proper dinner I'd had in a while and honestly probably the best in my life the potato was so soft and buttery and the cheese oozed over every inch of my meal. The lettuce by the side was crunchy and sweet and even the tomatoes where surprisingly delicious.I thanked everyone as did Zelvena and soon we were back in our room. We flopped onto our beds to let are stomachs settle. "That was so good!" I smile and Zelevena turns her head , "Welcome to Darkveil , told you we aren't all about eating blood for breakfast lunch and tea."We laugh again for a little Soon the sun slowly sets and it's not dark outside the moons glowing and I'm still talking to Zelvena. "So it's really gunna happen? The Charlotte thing""Yep, Tomorrow"The chat slowly fades and by now we are both in our pyjamas but Zelvenas weren't quite what I expected , judging by her black lace outfit in the daytime I expected quite formal looking black pyjamas but she wasn't she was dressed in a white top with white shirts with black stars all over , where I was just with a faded grey cosy T shirt and shorts. She looked sweet , I looked like a disaster but oh well.

When we awoke the next day the sun was beaming through the curtains even though they were closed . It closed up the room and I rubbed my eyes. Zelvena was awake but not up and dressed . Not long after we were both ready she was dressed in a black vest top with a thick leather jacket and black ripped jeans to match she threw on her tough leather boots and turned her head to me , just casual me."You ready?""You make it seem like an action movie were we are going to kick some serious butt" I smile "We are.... Charlottes butt to be exact" she flickered her pearly white fangs that struck down like daggers I knew Charlotte was going to be ripped to shreds like paper. And I didn't know how I felt about it.

Soon (17)

So Zelvena and I start walking out of those big brown doors I had been nervous to enter and once we'd found some trees she grabbed my hands and the purple mist swarmed round my feet and continued upwards untill I could see nothing else , however once it had faded we were standing outside school."You will have to go in now if you don't want to be late, meet Charlotte outside maths like she said, do not give her any money and if she's threatens to beat you up if you don't give her it , stand your ground and ask to take this so called fight outside" I nod as the instructions are flooding into my brain."Remember Holly, I'm right outside and I know what's going on , Good luck" she squeezed my hands tightly then let go and smiled the same sweet smile she showed when I had first met her with her black lips as her black midnight hair tumbled down her shoulders like some kind of Vampire Princess , hm wonder if they have those. "See you later" I blurt nervously and run down the schools steps and right through until I reach maths. She's not there yet so I wait nervously by the door. What do I do if her gang grabs hold of me before I can tell them to take the fight outside? I can't take all four of them on. Zelvena would come obvoiusly , but what if she punches me in a weird spot and knocks me out before Zelven- She's walking up the steps her golden flow of hair has been platted and gently placed over her shoulder , she's getting closer and I can see her bright pink lipstick that's been plastered into her lips and soon she's facing me with Rosie , Mia and Lilly behind her they all glare at me. Remember what she said Holly stand your ground."Aw look the trampy freak came girls, come on then I don't have all day hand over the money""No""Beg your pardon rat?"She cackled and looked at her friends who were giggling "Ohhh you think you can mess me about don't you freak? I'll give you one more chance before you get hurt.""Give me the money" she snarls "I said no" I repeat calmly.She jerks her arm out and grabs my collar and shoves me against the wall I panicked and shoved my foot into her stomach and she stumbled back , co fused by the fact I'd retaliated. She snarled up at me "You didn't just do that" she spat"If we are going to fight do it outside, that way you can't get caught and have your little reputation ruined" I glare back at the group who turn to each other and discuss it quickly. Everyone and then I could make out whispers like "Well that way if she ends up like that goth boy , no one will know it's me" I could see her smirking she turned back round to face me.She grabbed my collar again and dragged me down the steps she was moving so quickly it was all a blur she quickly walked out of the double doors until she reached the school gates they were locked but nobody guarded them. Big tall metal gates."Climb over tramp, NOW"As much as I didn't want to climb the gates no matter what Charlotte said I still had to , to get to Zelvena.I grabbed the cold metal in my hands and pulled myself up until I could slot my foot into a gap. I was struggling and Charlotte could see it , they were sniggering. I was ready to collapse at the top because I couldn't pull my self properly up and over. Then I felt some kind of magic tingle in my legs and they ever so slightly levitated so I couldn't feel the cold rough metal underneath them however not high enough for the others to notice. I quickly swung my legs over the side and whispered"Zelvena if you can hear me, I'm going to jump , jump down I need you to stop me just before I hit the floor then let me drop." I didn't have long I knew I had to jump I couldn't climb down because I'd be sure to slip and fall anyway it wasn't high enough that I'd die , but high enough where I'd break my leg. I pushed back of the gate and dropped a huge whoosh of air flew past my head and for a second I was so scared I let a small quick scream , but Zelvenas magic stopped me just before I hit the bottom but I pretend to fall a little to make it look real."Thank you" I whispered.

Enough (18)

"Your turn then" I shout from the other side of the fence. They giggle "what a stupid ugly beast" Like is that meant to be an insult really? Like stupid ugly beast? You can do better then that. "Think I'm going to break one of my rose- a-glow nails going over that fence!" Charlotte sniggers They go to the end of the gate where there's a thin gap. "Mia , you know what to do" One of the other girls kick the gate and a screw falls out which allows Charlotte to make the gap wider, wide enough for her to walk through effortlessly. I scoff, wow should have known she'd be too petty to climb over. But that didn't matter , at least we were both outside and I was closer to Zelvena. "Here, found a nice spot to have a fight" I say and we walk to a grassy, area with some trees. "You mean for you to die" I laugh sarcastically "Haha! She thinks I'm joking.... tell her girls tell her what happened to the last person that got on the wrong side of me" Another one of the girls started to talk "she pushed him and he-" "Fell backwards and hit his head on the curb , killing him" I say sternly. They all look at me "Your an Evil psychopath , and not one of the cool ones. Your dangerous," I turn to face her "gang" "And soon she'll turn on you, what if she asks for money and you don't have it , what if she pulls your hair , that leads to a punch, then a fight then the next minute , you end up like that poor boy. Dead" The girls look at each other then stare at Charlotte "Oh please , you really believe that?! Like I'd ever turn on you guys."The girls back up a tiny bit "Mia?! Rosie? , lily?!"They run , and they don't stop running until there well out of sight. Charlotte screams at them "LIKE ID EVER LIKE YOU GUYS ANYWAY, THERES PLENTY MORE PEOPLE WHO CAN REPLACE YOU" I just stare at her taking in everything that's happening. "Why do you always ruin things?! That's what you do isn't it! Isn't that why your mum left you? Because she didn't like you! Because you make things worse because your just another stupid freak"Normally whatever she said id learnt to ignore but when somebody talks about my mum in a bad way I see red. How dare she talk about my mother like that. How dare she.

"My Mother didn't leave me because she wanted to""Why then tramp? Ohh was she put into prison? That wouldn't surprise me" " I don't know why she left! But she didn't go to jail! She had to leave for something! It's none of your business!""Aww , " she sniggered " pressing some buttons am i?""Bet your mother couldn't even look at you, bet she was disappointed, bet she was ashamed of the fact you where her daughter because I mean, look at you. Why would anyone want you. Even your own mother left you Holly!"I could feel my tears sitting in my eyes making the world around me blurry I sat quietly because I guess she was right...,She came over to me and grabbed my neck tightly and jerked my head up."Even your own mother...."I grabbed her hair and yanked it as hard as I could her head jolted right and her neck twisted in the direction my hand was pulling.Like hell was she right."Nobody talks about my mother like that, NOBODY! MY MOTHER WAS A BILLION TIMES BETTER THEN THE WOMAN WE COULD EVER DREAM TO BE!" "SHE WASN'T EVER THERE""Of course she was! Think I got along through my life telling myself she's gone forever?! No! NO! I held on to the fact that she would always be in my heart, and not you, nor anyone could take that away from me!" I slapped her hard across the face and my hand print had marked a deep red stain across her face. She punched me across my jaw and it stung like mad but this wasn't the time to be weak. I saw Zelvena flicker down from wherever she was hiding. Charlotte did to."The hell did she come from?! Who is she, I'll kill her too! I swear down Holly! I'm done with you. Your dead! And nobody's going to care!"Zelvena flickerd to her in the blink of an eye and wrapped her icy fingers gently around her neck then dug in sharply. "I don't think so , not this time." She whispered in her ear."I hope this hurts you to hell , because you took my friend , I shan't let you take another"

It all happened so fast her mouth slowly widened until her giant fangs showed. She tried to scream but it was too late Zelvena had already plunged her fangs into her and began to suck the life out of her. And drop by drop the colour from her face slowly drained up into Zelvenas body. I watched her look like she was deflating In front of me I saw her skin shrivel around her bones. I saw the fear in her eyes and then she dropped she just collapsed like a frail sculpture her body was laid across the path. She looked so delicate. Little did everyone know how deadly she was.

Chaos (19)

I just stared at her for a little while, is just helped kill Charlotte Mannor. The girl who got away with everything. I didn't know whether it was right still, on one hand she was a bully but did she deserve to die? But then what about Sattrick she killed him! And me? She was going to kill me... so in a way it was self defence well , Zelvena actually sucked the blood out of her body?

No I've decided. I can't feel bad and I won't. She had it coming. Zelvena looked up at me , not with worry in her eyes or fear or as if she thought it was a mistake. Her expression was comforting and she stepped over to wrap her cold arms around me. I hugged her tightly back as the tears were now flooding out and I didn't even try stopping them."It's okay, Holly it's okay, she gone now, its all going to be okay""S-she was going to k-kill me Zelvena" I blubber into her shoulder "But she didn't , I wouldn't let her, not now , not ever.""What happens now?" I sat wiping the tears with my sleeve. I don't care what anyone says. Somebody could give me a tissue and I'd still wipe my Tears with my sleeve. "I don't know-

BZZZZZ BZZZZ BZZZZ BZZZZ "What the hell? I shove my hand into my pocket and pull out my phone." Dad. Dads calling."Do I answer it?!" I panic. Zelvena nods , so I do I put the cold phone to my ear and whisper

"Hello?""Holly?!" I hear dads voice, he sounds cold and tired and a little scared."Yeah? , d-dad it's me , what-what's up?""I promised your-""You promised mum you'd take care of me.... yeah well there's no need go do what you want dad, I've found people that want me , for who I am""Oh shut up blubbering Holly! Were have you been!""Just someplace""I need to see you right now!" He shouts, the one thing I'd never miss, his shout ing."Dad I'm not coming home!"He sighs angrily " it's not about that!"I have him on speaker and we both listen to him shouting nastily."Then what dad what could possibly be so important that you call nearly 2 days later?!" "Meet me at the coffee shop in 10 minutes Holly , I mean it." I thought about it for a second , we could always leave if he's talking rubbish , run out , hide behind a tree and let the purple mist take us back to Darkveil."Fine , but I'm bringing my friend.""What friend?!""You either accept it , or I don't come at all" "Since when did you start giving orders and taking charge?!" He shouts"Since you forgot to step up and take care of your daughter""Well it's not my fault if your - ""What dad? , say it... strange!""Well, yes but-""Cafe , 10 minutes , you me and my friend. Take it or leave it"He sighs and I hang up.

"Some times I wish I could suck all of his blood"I look at her"Two far?" We smile a little . Charlottes body is still laying there. Zelvena clicks her fingers and she disappears."Where'd you put her?" I ask nervously "At home , on her bed"There wasn't much more to say so we walk down to the coffee shop and walk in , the smell of cinnamon floods into my lungs. I'd missed that smell so much we ordered two coffees. I bought them this time. Two cinnamon lattes. We sat down at a table in the corner and waited. Dad came in the door in a big coat , panting , saw us and stumbled over to us, sat down and took of his big coat."Well , what do you want?" I sigh He glares at Zelvena. She sits there and glared back, she doesn't even flinch."Who's this then." He points rudely at her."That's my friend Zelvena" I reply"Zelvena? What kind of a name is th-""She's been there for me more in the last few days then you have in my life so don't you dare start to pick on her or make her feel like she's worthless" I speak sternly and I glare at him. He turns to me but keeps quiet."What the hell did you want me for.""Where have you been""Oh not this again! Dad I've been with Zelvena! Okay? I'm safe aren't I? "He glares at Zelvena and starts to talk to her. He's shaking a little and he's pointing at her "I know , who you are! What you do. Your a cold blooded killer Aren't you? ..... AREN'T YOU?!" Some People in the cafe Turn to see who's shouting then turn back round and continue drinking there coffees."I'm sorry sir , I don't understand" she keeps the still, stern look on her face"Dad leans closer and spits his words through gritted teeth "Don't play dumb with me, you stupid -Your A vampire!"Dad knew. All along he'd known and he hadn't said a word"WHAT?! Dad!! How - how do you know?..."

www.ingramcontent.com/pod-product-compliance
Lightning Source LLC
Chambersburg PA
CBHW071358200726
48294CB00004B/1214